INCUR

BY

CHRISTOPHER JOYCE

Chapter One

Space is cold.

Archer knew this, of course; everybody knew this. What he didn't know was how the fuck it could be even colder *inside* the ship. He pulled a thick blanket close, squeezing his knees in tight and tucking the wool under his chin, and he shook the thought out of his tired mind. His quarters were small and sparsely decorated, but they were comfortable. He had a bathroom, a bed, some books, and an entertainment system he could use to play music, games, or puzzles if he wanted, but he rarely used it. As necessary as space flight was to his job - intrinsic, really - it didn't mean he had to like it, and he found himself frustrated at the incessant waiting.

Archer and the rest of the expeditionary crew had boarded the research shuttle the *Crimson Jackal* three standard weeks earlier, and the shuttle had, in turn, docked with the much larger capital cruiser *Imperious* in order to make short work of a long journey. Archer and co. had never left the shuttle, never ventured aboard the *Imperious* herself, never rubbed shoulders with the rest of the crew and researchers so many levels above their heads. They were scientists, not tourists, as Bordello was wont to say. So they stayed on the *Jackal*, and kept to themselves.

Finally, they were close enough to their destination that the *Jackal* would shortly disengage from the bowels of the *Imperious* and begin a manual descent to the target planet below.

Archer kicked off the blanket in frustration and checked his watch.

Plenty of time yet.

He jumped off the bed and jogged on the spot for a few moments, trying to warm himself up and get the blood flowing once more. Satisfied, and a little out of breath, he made his way to the small table in the corner of his quarters upon which were piled numerous charts, maps, scribbled notes, and detailed annotated drawings. He selected a particular star map and furrowed his brow as he scrutinised it for the hundredth time.

Planet C13-J7, more commonly known as Andani; fourth planet from the yellow star Capra in the Fomori cluster.

He knew these details by heart, of course, but felt compelled to read them again anyway. He nodded, and put the map down. Next, he cross-referenced the planetary information against a copy of the official mission brief they'd been given.

Atmosphere within breathable range (tolerance - 3.5%)

Structures of interest at coordinates provided overleaf.

No indication of intelligent life.

Try as he might, Archer just couldn't seem to shake a feeling of vague, half-formed unease at that last part. He was a xenoarchaeologist by trade, an intelligent man, so the idea that a planet which was purportedly home to monoliths, stone circles, and other such examples of neolithic alien architecture did not contain intelligent life, was something of a contradiction in terms to Archer, and it worried him; it worried him a lot.

A loud, shrill *ping* rang out across the ship's comm systems; whilst Archer usually found the sound loathsome, he knew what it meant this time and his spirits were lifted somewhat by the implication.

"All crew to the cockpit in fifteen minutes," came the electronic voice over the speaker. Archer didn't mind Medd, their onboard medical and maintenance mech; in fact, he had grown quite fond of the damn thing, though he would never admit it.

Alright, Archer thought as he zipped up his flight jacket and secured his heavy boots.

Here we go.

He left his quarters without so much as a backwards glance, and made his way through the twisting and winding corridors which led to the common area of the shuttle, terminating in the cockpit. The *Jackal* was utilitarian at best; all blinking lights, steel panelling, and exposed pipes and wires. It lacked the sleek lines and pleasant decor of its parent the *Imperious*, but a crew of four scientists and a mech were unlikely to scoff at the aesthetics.

"Morning buddy," came a voice from Archer's left as he entered the wide, roughly circular common area. He turned to see an equally tired looking Bordello - a fellow xenoarchaeologist - waving a hot coffee in his direction.

"Thanks, man," said Archer, gratefully accepting the drink.

"Hey," said the biologist and botanist Chan from her seat at the table.

"Morning guys," added astrophysicist and rookie pilot Ivy from hers.

Archer and Bordello joined their colleagues at the table. Each sat and sipped their respective drinks in near silence. At the far end of the common area stood a large steel door, the entrance to the cockpit. The indicator panel to the right of the door currently displayed a static red light.

The common area housed a modest and very heavily reinforced viewport, and one by one the crew members looked up from their mugs to glimpse the stars which blinked and burned beyond the small window. By degrees, the sliver of space they could see through the viewport began to take on a lighter hue; shades of yellow and orange just visible at the outer edges.

"The sun must be coming up," said Ivy, "we must be here."

As if on cue, another electronic *beep* sounded, and the red light on the cockpit door indicator panel turned green. The door slid open with a *whoosh*, and a draft of warm air was blown into the common area.

"This way, please," called Medd from the pilot's seat. The four crew did as instructed and made their way into the cockpit. Archer never failed to be impressed by the array of buttons, panels, electronic displays, and myriad other intricacies of the spacious cockpit, though he had little to no idea what the fuck any of it actually did.

That's what Medd's here for, he often said.

He strapped himself in at the mech's instruction, and made himself as comfortable as he was able. With everyone now secured and ready, Medd began his work. A series of buttons were pressed, a number of dials turned, and a selection of levers were pulled. Then, with a deep rumble and a stomach-turning lurch, the *Jackal* disengaged from the *Imperious*. The shuttle seemed to simply sit there, untethered and floating, for a long moment before Medd engaged the thrusters and the *Jackal* burst into motion.

If the view from the small viewport in the common area had been impressive, then the sight currently coming into focus in front of them through the large panoramic forward canopy could only be described as majestic.

The planet Andani filled the entire field of view, and a halo of light cast the scene in gold as the star Capra announced itself on the far side of the planet.

"We should reach the designated landing zone in approximately two hours and eight minutes," said Medd. The crew nodded their respective understanding, and continued to watch as the burgeoning sun revealed more of the planet. It appeared mainly brown from their current vantage point, with some red areas scattered here and there. The poles appeared lighter, but their exact composition was so far unknown.

Another job for another day, thought Archer as he watched the planet slowly grow in his field of vision, revealing more of its secrets with every kilometre they hurtled toward it.

The crew were silent as they stared down at the strange and fascinating planet, blissfully unaware that something else was staring right back.

Chapter Two

Medd was right about their descent time, of course; he was a machine, he rarely got such things wrong. In fact, Archer couldn't recall a time that the mech had actually been wrong about anything, which was mildly annoying.

As the *Jackal* slowed to a crawl and began its final descent to the rocky ground below, Archer noticed for the first time just how warm it had gotten once they had broken through Andani's atmosphere.

Good, he thought; *that ship was fucking freezing.*

The *Jackal* came to a stop on the surface, and Medd ran through all of the final checks before powering down the shuttle.

"It is now safe to unbuckle yourselves," said the mech, and the crew wasted no time in doing just that. As each of the four humans stood from their flight seats, they stretched their respective legs, and clicked their respective backs; space flight was not an altogether comfortable business.

"Okay," said Archer, "the sun is coming up, so we have plenty of daylight ahead of us. Suit up, grab your shit, and meet me in the hangar at-" he checked his watch, "oh-nine-hundred."

"Roger that," came the collective reply from Bordello, Ivy, and Chan.

*

The team was well-drilled, and as such were assembled, kitted up, and ready to go before the allotted time, which pleased Archer. He was not the captain, per se, but as the oldest and most experienced member of the crew, the others looked up to him and were more than happy to follow his lead. Technically speaking, the highest ranking member of the crew was Medd; the four humans aboard were essentially scientists, but Medd was property of Collected Systems Governance, which gave him the higher rank.

Archer was pleased to find his team ready, and even more pleased to see that they were already loading the equipment into the lander when he arrived. A small, relatively uncomfortable machine with four large wheels, the transport was rugged enough to handle uneven and uncharted terrain, with just enough room for scientific equipment, medical supplies, and weapons. Archer often lamented the mandated inclusion of firearms on mission; they were researchers, explorers, academics, all, three weeks of basic weapons training notwithstanding. He did acknowledge, however, albeit grudgingly, that they simply did not know what to expect now that they had made planetfall.

The remote probes which had first identified this planet as a *destination of interest* had scanned the planet, and relayed images taken from orbit which appeared to show monoliths, standing stone circles, and other curious structures which Collected Systems Governance had subsequently marked as high-priority targets for a manned research mission. What the probes had not detected, however, at least on a visual level, was any sign of life, let alone a sophisticated civilisation.

Someone built those structures, though, or some thing, thought Archer, thus justifying the firearms, at least to himself. Chan, however, was not convinced; she had never been convinced. A true pacifist at heart, Chan was - perhaps ironically - openly hostile to the inclusion of weapons on a research mission.

Fucking biologists, Archer thought, though not entirely seriously.

"Okay, are we ready? Medd?" he called out to the crew.

"All systems functional, and supply transfer complete," Medd confirmed.

"All set, boss-man," came the reply from Bordello, complete with an ironic salute.

"Okay then," Archer replied, nodding. "Let's go. Take us out, Medd."

"Affirmative," replied the mech, as he fired up the lander. He hit a button on the dashboard, and the *Crimson Jackal*'s boarding ramp began to open, casting bright, morning sunlight into the otherwise grey and utilitarian hangar.

With rumble and a lurch, the lander zipped forward at a velocity which belied its boxy and ungainly aspect, and as the tyres hit the dirt beyond the boarding ramp, Archer and the crew were granted their first real look at the planet.

The surface was an uneven blanket of oranges, reds, and browns; it appeared to be an arid planet, and the humidity in the air lent credence to this assumption. But the vegetation did not. Littered here and there at regular intervals as far as they could see, stood tall, green plants which appeared to be thriving despite the harsh landscape in which they stood. Their stems were thick and strong, and each of the myriad varieties of plant life they could see as they passed at speed appeared to sport evolutionary defence mechanisms; spikes, traps, hooks, thorns - Archer would be more than happy to never see these lush, green things up close.

Chan, however, thought differently.

"Look at how green that one is," she said, pointing to a thick-stemmed plant of some exotic kind which was, admittedly, a bright, vivid shade of green.

"And that one; did you see how sharp those spines were? And how red? Man… There must be water just below the surface; lots of water, judging by these beauties," Her camera recorded image after image of the strange, alien vegetation, and Archer couldn't help but smile a little in spite of himself.

Fucking botanists…

Archer checked the readout on his CSG-issue portable device, which currently showed a topographic scan of Andani's surface, counting down the distance to their first objective as they hurtled along in the lander, bumping and bouncing in concert with the peaks and troughs of the uneven surface. His stomach gave an uncomfortable lurch, which Archer knew had less to do with the uneven ground and more to do with the burgeoning feeling of unease he was beginning to feel. Though it was more subconscious than overt, he definitely felt it, and the feeling seemed to be increasing in potency the closer they drew to their initial destination.

He cast a glance around the lander; Medd was driving, of course, his metallic, angular 'shoulders' visible at the edges of the driver's seat. Ivy and Bordello were deep in conversation as they checked the mission briefing one final time, absorbing as much as they could from the limited resources CSG had made available. Chan was in her element, and her camera clicked, clicked, and clicked again as she catalogued as much of the alien greenery as she could at their current speed.

Everyone seems fine, Archer thought. *It's probably nothing.*

He checked his device once more, and cleared his throat.

"All right," he called out. "Look alive, people; distance to *Priority One*: two kilometres."

The crew stopped what they were doing, and ran final visual checks on their equipment and weapons. Satisfied, each in turn steeled themselves and either nodded or gave a thumbs-up in Archer's direction. Minutes later, a descending mechanical whirl announced that the lander was slowing down, and the crew stood as one as Medd brought the vehicle to a dead stop.

"*Priority One*, reached," announced Medd, ever one for stating the obvious. The mech hit the door release button on the main control console, and the lander door slid open. With Archer on point, the crew stepped out onto the surface of the planet, and were immediately conscious of just how humid it was. But they did not openly acknowledge this, nor pay it any mind at all. To a man and woman, all of the crew's attention was focused ahead, and up. Inside their protective helmets, jaws hung open and throats gulped nervously. It was Bordello who spoke first, giving voice to the words they were all thinking.

"Holy mother of fuck," said the xenoarchaeologist, as he stared up at the imposing, dark stone obelisk which towered over them, casting a long, deep shadow over the uneven ground beneath their feet.

"My god," added Ivy. "It must be over two-hundred feet tall."

"At least," added Archer, as he took a cautious step closer. The feeling in his gut had not dissipated; quite the opposite in fact.

"Two hundred and thirty seven, to be exact," added Medd as he came up to join the four humans. Archer checked his portable device, looking specifically at the live atmospheric readout. Satisfied, he signalled to the group, calling for their attention.

"Alright, people," he said, already beginning the process of removing his helmet, "I'll leave it up to each of you; personal choice. But I'm taking this fucking thing off."

"Thank the sweet baby Jesus for that," said Bordello, not needing a second invitation. Ivy and Chan followed suit; after all, it would be much easier to work without the restriction of the bulky helmets. Now free of the headgear, each of the crew took a long, deep lungfull of the alien air.

"What do you suppose those mean?" asked Chan, turning back to the imposing structure, and waving her hand to indicate countless intricately carved symbols and glyphs which covered the surface of the monolith.

"Never mind what they mean," replied Bordello, walking closer, "should they be glowing like that?"

Archer had not registered this at first, so dumbstruck was he at the sight of the thing in all its glory. But

Bordello was right; as he took a step, then another, toward the massive standing stone, he could see the faint, ethereal glow which seemed to emanate from within the monolith, visible through the lines and curves of the carvings upon its surface.

"Medd?" said Archer over his shoulder, not turning to look at the mech.

"Yes, Doctor?" replied the faithful machine.

"Can you run a scan on this thing? Find out what sort of energy it's outputting?"

"Of course, sir. At first glance, it does not appear too dissimilar to the light radiated by certain strains of iridescent algae, but a more thorough scan would indeed provide a more robust and conclusive data set."

"Algae?" Chan interjected. "Are you saying there's something alive inside this thing?"

"As I have said, ma'am, I would require a more intensive assessment in order to provide a definitive conclusion. But in short, *yes* - though only in a certain manner of speaking."

"Fuck," said Archer under his breath, before finding his voice. "Alright, guys, don't forget we have a job to do here. You all know your roles, and everything we need is in the lander. So grab your shit and get to work; the light won't hold forever." He turned and looked up once more at the tall, foreboding monolith, "and we need to find out exactly what the fuck this thing is."

And who built it, he added voicelessly.

Chapter Three

It was easy to lose track of time aboard the *Jackal*, especially when it was docked with the much larger *Imperious*, hurtling through open space at speeds once considered achievable by even the most brilliant human minds. But to lose track of time whilst making the first ever human incursion onto the surface of an utterly alien planet like Andani, well, that took some doing. Such was the nature of the task in hand, however, and so engrossed were the four humans in question, that it took a timely reminder from Medd to bring their respective minds back to the here and now.

"We're losing the light," stated the mech. "I would advise dismantling the equipment and returning to the *Crimson Jackal* without delay."

"Copy that, Medd," replied Archer, looking up from the screen of his portable device upon which was displayed an ultra-magnified image of a piece of the imposing monolith he had been able to chip off with a small hand-axe.

"Alright, you heard him. Pack this shit up and let's move out."

"Um, Archer?" said Ivy, a little tentatively.

"Yeah?"

"There's so much here," she said with a sweeping gesture which took in the landscape and the monolith, "there's still so much we can learn."

"Your point?" replied Archer, the words coming out a little sharper than he had intended. This sting seemed to galvanise Ivy, who raised her eyebrows pointedly before replying.

"My *point* is that we've barely scratched the surface. We can't leave just because it's getting dark."

"Believe me," replied Archer, forcing more of a conciliatory tone into his voice, "I know just as well as anyone else that thing is a fucking *goldmine*." He threw a thumb over his shoulder, as if the massive and foreboding standing stone needed to be pointed out.

"But if Medd says it's time to leave, then *it's time to leave.* Copy?"

Ivy did not immediately reply, but held her ground even as she held his gaze. A long moment passed, and Ivy let out a sigh.

"Copy."

"Alright then," replied Archer, "and hey, don't worry; we'll be back here at first light to pick up right where we left off."

Nods of approval, and an obligatory mock-salute from Bordello, greeted Archer's words, and the team set about dismantling and packing away their equipment. Satisfied, Archer turned to the mech.

"Hey, Medd?" he called.

"Yes, Doctor Archer?" replied the cumbersome and inelegant mech. Archer had wondered on more than one occasion why CSG insisted on using the ungainly mechanicals instead of the more sleek and human-looking androids which were ubiquitous throughout the Collected Systems; it's not like they couldn't afford them. Shaking the stray thought from his head, Archer brandished his portable device in the boxy, utilitarian mech's direction.

"What do you make of this?" he said, angling the display toward what passed for Medd's face. The mech took the data pad and scrutinised the data. Beside the magnified image was a readout of elements which the device had identified as being present in Archer's sample.

"I would need to perform a more thorough and robust series of tests aboard the *Crimson Jackal* in order to be certain, Doctor, but from this initial data, I would conclude that this monolith is made of-"

"Rock," interjected Archer. "Right? Just plain old, fucking, rock - like we have back on Earth. Correct?"

"Yes," replied Medd, simply. Archer shook his head slowly.

"It doesn't make sense," he said aloud, more to himself than to Medd. "Where we are; the distance we've come… I expected… I don't know. I expected something more-"

"Alien?" said Medd. Archer merely nodded, looking off into the distance.

*

Thirty minutes later, they were packed up and ready to go. Archer and Bordello were busy loading the equipment onto the lander, whilst Ivy and Chan were taking whatever time they had to look at, touch, and image the monolith.

"Doctor Chan, ma'am?" said Medd. Chan either did not hear the mech, or heard him and
Chose to ignore the electronic voice which emanated from Medd's speakers.

"Doctor Chan?" the mech repeated, louder this time.

"What is it, Medd?" the biologist replied.

"I have detected a lifeform within our sector. Something large."

The crew was immediately on alert, and rounded on Medd.

"*How* large?" asked Chan, who had covered the distance between herself and the mech in two long strides.

"Approximately seven feet in height, ma'am; equally wide, with what I believe to be six limbs, possibly eight."

"You got all that from a sensor scan?" asked Chan.

"No, Doctor, of course not." Medd raised his arm and extended a metal finger toward a point in the near-distance, behind the crew.

"It's right over there."

*

"Everybody, fall back!" came the command from Archer as he, Bordello, and Ivy drew their weapons and adopted firing stances. Their crosshairs were trained on the thing which had appeared, quite suddenly, from the other side of a natural ridge. Archer had never seen anything like it before, and the most immediate analogue his mind could summon in that alarming instant was some variation of the common crab or lobster, but far bigger and bluer in hue. It had four thick, powerful-looking legs which terminated in what appeared to be claws, rather than feet; two additional fore-limbs, however, much more closely resembled arms and sported long, thin finger-like tendrils at their extreme ends. Its neck was long, sloping upwards like that of a brachiosaur, but its head and face were utterly alien.

Archer could see the creature's eyes, even from this distance, and he swore that they were staring right at him.

"No!" shouted Chan, jumping in front of her colleagues, and spreading her arms wide. "Don't shoot!"

"Are you out of your fucking mind?" Bordello shouted back, "look at the size of that thing!"

"It's not doing anything," Chan protested, "It's not a threat!"

Archer only had a moment to decide. Whatever he did next would define the mission, for good or ill, and he only had a split second to make his decision.

"Move, Chan. Right now," he commanded.

"Archer, no," she pleaded, recognising the resolve in his eyes.

"Right now, Chan," he repeated, "or I'll report this to Command as insubordination."

Chan held her ground. She turned her back on her team and faced the creature on the ridge. Her arms were still held out by her sides, palms raised. She took a step toward the creature, then another.

"Chan! For fuck sake!" Bordello called out to his colleague. But she wasn't listening. Her eyes were fixed on the strange creature ahead of her. She had not actually expected to find true sentient life on Andani, let alone the magnificent thing she was now slowly walking towards. As for the alien itself, it had not given any indication that it intended to move any closer to the four humans and their mech, but merely cocked its head to one side inquisitively in a very human gesture as Chan approached. Chan recognised all too well that they were just as unfamiliar to the creature as it was to them. She inched closer, ignoring the protests which persisted behind her, but stopped abruptly when the creature moved.

It raised one of its arms, and spread its thin fingers out toward Chan, taking a step forward as it did so. Chan was so enraptured that she did not hear Bordello's hasty approach, and as such was wholly unprepared for the impact as he tackled her to the ground from behind.

"Now!" came Bordello's cry, and the unmistakable sound of automatic gunfire rang out from somewhere behind the now prone Chan.

The sound of gunfire ceased after ten seconds or so, and Bordello released his grip on Chan at Archer's command. The biologist regained her feet, and immediately turned to look at the creature. Her fears were confirmed as she gazed upon its bullet-riddled body; she rounded on her colleagues.

"How could you? It meant us no harm! You fucking *murdered* it. Do you realise how much we could have learned from-"

"Doctors," Medd cut in. Even though his voice was a mere mechanical construct, the crew could not fail to notice the urgency it conveyed.

"What is it, Medd?" called Archer, his adrenaline through the roof following the events of the last few minutes.

"There are more of them," the mech replied, simply. The crew turned as one, and cries of 'fall back' rang out as they beheld another of the creatures appear over the ridge, then another, then another, then another, until there were at least thirty or forty of the things in sight. Their behaviour was noticeably different to that of the previous creature, and Chan had no doubt that this shift in temperament was a direct result of the rash actions of her team. The creatures were agitated - one did not have to be a xenobiologist to recognise that much - and as if reacting to some unseen, unspoken cue, the assembled creatures raised their arms, fingers stretching and groping in the approximate direction of the humans, and they ran.

"The lander!" shouted Archer, indicating a full retreat, and the crew ran. They did not turn and fire, nor did they waste time taking up alternating firing positions - one laying down fire whilst the others retreated - they simply turned and ran as fast as their suits would allow in the direction of their transport.

"Haul ass, Ivy," Archer called over his shoulder to the physicist turned trainee pilot. The youngest member of the crew, Ivy was also the smallest, and she was already starting to lag behind. The lander wasn't far, only a few hundred metres from the monolith, but it was far enough.

Archer made it to the vehicle first, practically ripping the door from its hinges as he yanked it open, waving his team inside. Medd took up his position at the controls, and Chan and Bordello were only moments behind the mech, throwing themselves into the open vehicle. Both immediately turned, weapons drawn, to face back outside in time to see Ivy trip a mere fifty or so yards from the safety of the lander. She did not fall to the ground, but her stumble cost her precious seconds.

And that was all they needed.

Archer, Bordello, and Chan watched in horror as a set of long, sinewy fingers came into view behind Ivy, and closed tightly around her skull.

The others were barely even aware of their own screams as they watched the creature clutching Ivy by the head. Bordello closed one eye and squinted down the barrel of his rifle, but there was no shot; at this distance he would surely hit Ivy. There was nothing they could do. Long moments played out in near silence, with nothing but the sound of their own pulses thundering in their ears.

"Wait," said Chan at length. She furrowed her brow and placed one hand on the open doorway, pulling herself out of the vehicle ever so slightly to gain a better view of the scene.

"Chan-" Archer began, but the biologist waved away his words.

"What the fuck is it doing?" Chan said, as she watched the creature still clutching Ivy by the head. It did not squeeze; it did not tear; it did not drag or toss; it appeared to simply be holding onto her.

"Look at the others," Chan added. It was only then that Archer and Bordello saw what Chan was seeing - the rest of the creatures were holding their positions behind the one in whose grasp Ivy remained. They had ceased chasing the crew, and gave no indication that they were about to resume their pursuit.

After what seemed like an age, the creature let go of Ivy, and retreated; they all retreated, moving backwards away from Ivy and back toward the ridge.

"Ivy!" called Archer, waving frantically for her to join them in the lander. "Come on!"

Ivy did not move. She remained rooted to the spot, despite the creatures having now retreated back beyond the ridge. Her eyes seemed to regain focus, and she set her jaw, stoically. Although there was some distance between her and Archer, she raised her head and met the team leader's uncomprehending stare with one of her own. The look in her eyes, though, was not one of panic, alarm, or pleading.

Archer began to register a dull, dark feeling in the pit of his stomach, and he fought hard to quell the burgeoning dread which threatened to consume him.

The look in Ivy's eyes, to Archer's dawning horror, was one of sorrow, a deep, pure sorrow, and behind it, *resolve*.

"Ivy-" Archer began, his voice faltering as he tried in vain to forestall what he somehow knew was coming. Still holding Archer's gaze, Ivy gave a small, sad shake of her head.

In one lightning-fast movement, she took out her sidearm, placed it to her temple, and pulled the trigger.

Archer did not remember falling to the floor, nor did he react to the deep rumble and mechanical din as Medd engaged the lander's engines. All that his reeling mind could focus on was the sight of Ivy's blood, now indistinguishable from the red-brown dirt into which her body had fallen.

Chapter Four

"What the fuck are you doing, you mechanical piece of shit?"

The sound of Bordello's voice brought Archer back to himself, snapping him out of the state of shock he had found himself in since Ivy pulled the trigger. He shook his head to clear his mind, and registered Chan's hand around his arm, hauling him to his feet. Bordello was screaming at Medd to *stop the fucking vehicle and turn it the fuck around*, and that was when Archer realised what was happening.

"Why are we moving?" Archer said as he gained his feet. "What's going on? Medd?"

"I am sorry, Doctor Archer, but as I have explained to Doctor Bordello, we must return to the *Crimson Jackal* at once."

"But what about Ivy? We can't just-"

"I repeat my apologies, Doctors, but we cannot delay. There is a storm approaching rapidly from the north east, and we must regain the safety of the ship."

"What sort of storm, Medd?" asked Chan. Her voice was distant, hollow; the events of the past - how long? She had no idea - had taken a toll on the biologist. The mech risked a glance over his shoulder and fixed Chan with his bright photoreceptors.

"A bad one," he replied.

The *Jackal* was now in sight, its lights guiding the lander as the darkness drew in. It had turned noticeably colder inside the lander, and from the small windows the remaining crew members could see the effects of the wind which was now swirling violently beyond the steel frame of their vehicle. Medd touched a button on the lander's centre console, and the *Jackal's* landing ramp began its descent. The mech did not slow the lander as it made its approach; he had timed it to perfection, as always, and simply drove the vehicle straight up the ramp and into the hangar before he finally disengaged the engines.

Nobody moved, and nobody spoke. The silence was as unbearable as it was understandable, and Medd knew enough about human emotion to allow Archer, Chan, and Bordello a moment of silent reflection whilst they caught their breaths and tried to figure out exactly what the fuck had just happened. But a moment was all the mech could spare, and he was soon forced to interrupt.

"My apologies, but we really must get back to the bridge," he said as delicately as he could.

Bordello turned and fixed Medd with a deathly stare, and Chan simply sat, elbows resting upon her knees, and she held her head as she stared at the riveted metal floor of the lander.

Archer took a deep breath and, finding both the strength and will from *somewhere*, stood.

"Come on, you heard him. On your feet, you two."

Bordello raised his head to meet Archer's gaze, but did not stand.

"What just happened, Archer? What the fuck were those things?"

"I don't know, pal," Archer replied, shaking his head, "but that's what we're gonna figure out - all of us. Together. Okay?"

Bordello took a deep breath, and ran his hands forcefully through his hair in a show of exasperation, then he stood.

"Chan?" he said, delicately. The biologist looked up at the sound of her name, and noted that she was the only one still sitting. She closed her eyes for a moment to centre herself, and then she too stood.

"Come on," she said, "let's go see about that storm."

*

The crew removed their environmental gear as quickly as they could, and were soon on the bridge in regular, infinitely more comfortable flight suits. Archer was happy to let Chan take the lead on the storm, as it seemed to be helping her to deal with Ivy's death. Archer did not immediately join the others on the bridge, but instead headed to his cabin to record some notes whilst the events of the last few hours were still fresh in his mind. He knew he would have to make an official report once the mission had concluded, and he did not want to miss a single detail.

On the bridge, Chan and Medd were a blur of activity.

"How bad is it, Medd? Talk to me," Chan said as she took up a position behind the mech whereby she could access the latest atmospheric data on myriad readouts and data feeds.

"Very high levels of sulphur dioxide, and even higher levels of nitrogen oxides, ma'am," said the mech as he studied a monitor.

"Shit," replied Chan, sighing heavily, "that's bad."

"I suggest we raise the shields," said Medd, receiving a nod of agreement from Chan.

"Whoa, hang on a second," interjected Bordello, who had until this point been sitting quietly at the communal table nursing a rather tall and rather neat whisky. "Please tell me you're not seriously suggesting staying planetside?"

"Indeed," replied Medd, still studying the various displays. "It is far too dangerous to take off in these conditions. Besides, we still have approximately seventy-six percent of our mission left to complete."

Bordello stood and slammed his fist down onto the table.

"Are you out of your fucking mind?" he shouted, pointing at Medd and Chan in turn. "We lost Ivy, and there are fucking creatures out there, big, hostile creatures - the variables have well and truly fucking *changed*."

"Not at all," replied Chan. "You know as well as I do that we can't simply abort the mission without the express consent of all active crew members. The decision to leave has to be unanimous, Bordello, that's the only way to override Medd's directives, and I for one am not going anywhere. Those things, whatever they are, they're not hostile."

Bordello raised his eyebrows pointedly, but did not immediately reply. The pair held each other's gaze for a long, tense moment.

"I'm sorry Chan," said Bordello at length, "I'm going to have to ask you to repeat that; for a moment there I could have sworn you said they *weren't hostile*."

"We've seen no evidence whatsoever that they mean us any harm," Chan replied. Bordello picked up his glass and hurled it forcefully at the wall, shattering it and raining shards of glass upon the floor.

"Hey, hey! What the fuck is going on in here?" asked Archer as he finally entered the bridge.

"Archer," said a bleary-eyed Bordello, "tell these fucking idiots that we have to leave, and leave now."

"We cannot leave, as I have explained," said Medd.

"Medd's right, Archer. We can't take off in this," said Chan.

"She's out of her mind, man," interjected Bordello, waving his hand roughly in Chan's direction. "Saying those things out there are all friendly and shit."

"I never said they were *friendly*, Bordello, but I don't think they're hostile either."

"Whoa, slow down, Chan," said Archer, raising his palms for calm. "What do you mean?

"Think about it," said the biologist. "The first one we saw, it was just watching us. It didn't attack, didn't growl or hiss, didn't bare its teeth, rear up, or do anything you would associate with lions, bears, or any other predatory animal on Earth. And then *you*," she raised a finger and pointed it accusingly at both Archer and Bordello, "shot it."

"It moved toward us with its arms raised, Chan," Archer argued.

"Yeah, it did," the biologist agreed. "You know what else does that? Toddlers. Puppies. Bear cubs. Do I need to go on? It wasn't a threat," she repeated defiantly, hands on hips.

"Yeah, sure," replied Bordello sarcastically, "which is why fifty of its friends showed up."

"Jesus… You're making my point *for me*, Bordello," said an exasperated Chan. "Fifty of its friends showed up, and what did they do? Nothing."

"Nothing? They killed Ivy!" shouted Bordello.

"Ivy killed *herself*!" Chan shouted back louder.

"Alright, that's enough out of the both of you," said Archer in a tone which brooked no argument. "We have no idea what the fuck we're up against here, and if we can't take off then I suggest we make this place defensible, just in case the worst should happen."

"No need," said Chan simply. "Medd: shields up, and max them out. Reroute the power from the weapon systems if you have to. That'll be enough to keep anything out, and it'll give us cover from the hellfire which is about to start pouring down on us. Now I suggest we all get some rest, we still have a mission to complete, and I for one intend to see it through." Chan turned and strode away from the bridge toward her cabin, swiping Bordello's whiskey bottle from the table as she went.

"She's fucking crazy, man," Bordello said to Archer once Chan was beyond earshot. "I say we fucking go; if we can't override Medd's fucking directives, why don't we just put a bullet in its head and get the fuck off this planet?"

"Slow down, pal; think it through. With Ivy gone, there's nobody left who could even pilot the ship. We need to see this through, if only for a while longer."

Medd engaged the energy shields which came immediately to life with an electronic whir, and the acid rain began to fall.

*

Chan did not immediately return to her quarters, but instead headed back toward the hangar in which Medd had earlier brought the lander to a skidding halt. It was dark, with only the artificial glare of low-powered strip lights offering any sort of illumination. It was quiet, too; only the soft, ambient hum of machinery, mingled with the infrequent tapping from the pipework and the chinking of chains and steel cables overhead, served to break the deathly silence.

Perfect, thought Chan as she took up a position atop one of the many supply crates which were stowed in the multipurpose hangar. She settled, and arched her back, eliciting a satisfying click from the base of her spine. She removed the top from Bordello's whisky bottle with a wry yet decidedly humourless grin.

Fuck him, she thought, *he can go find another one.*

She took a long swig from the bottle, and savoured the warm sting of the drink as it hit her throat. CSG supplies were shit, but at least the liquor was half decent.

And the coffee, Chan conceded to nobody but herself.

She sat a while longer, lost in her own mind, trying to make sense of what had happened that day but finding that she simply could not. She placed the bottle onto the floor and took a deep breath, closing her eyes as she exhaled. She felt her lip threatening to quiver, just a touch, barely even a tremor, but enough to know that her emotions were battling for the full attention of her fraught and exhausted mind. In that moment, she realised that now really wasn't the time for deep reflection on the day's events, and it certainly wasn't the time for any form of emotional self-analysis. No, now was the time to simply pick up Bordello's whisky, and get as drunk as f-

Thud.

Chan cocked her head to one side as she registered the sound. At least she thought she had registered something… Maybe she hadn't - these old ships with their ancient-

Thud.

This time she definitely heard it. She raised her chin and tried to focus her mind, listening out for the sound she had definitely heard but could not immediately place. She mentally checked off the sounds she *could* recognise: the low, barely perceptible hum of the ship's power cables; the metallic clinking from the ables above; she heard the crackle of the energy shield which protected the ship mere metres beyond the outer hull against which she leaned; she registered the constant, incessant pitter-patter of the acid rain as it fell all around, and the hissing it made as it hit the shield.

And through it all, under it all, a small, rhythmic thudding sound. Chan stood at once and moved to the nearest wall-mounted terminal. She hit a combination of keys with a practised grace and brought up a live feed from the *Jackal's* external cameras onto the display monitor.

"No way," she whispered out loud. "No fucking way."

She shook her head slowly as she continued to watch the live feed. "What *are* you up to?" Shutting down the feed for a moment, Chan instead brought up the internal comms system.

"Hey, Archer? You there?"

"Copy, Chan," came Archer's immediate response. "You okay?"

"Yeah, good; hey, listen," Chan responded, hurriedly. "You're not gonna believe this, but the locals are right outside."

"Locals? I'm sorry, you're gonna have to repeat that last part."

"The locals, the creatures. They're right outside the energy shield. I'll be damned," she added as a realisation dawned on her, "they must have evolved to withstand the acid rain."

Archer did not immediately reply, but Chan thought she could hear movement from the other end of the comms system. No doubt Archer had jumped up out of his chair to see for himself.

"Mother fuckers," Chan eventually heard Archer say.

"Okay Chan," he added, "stay put. Bordello and I will move to the armoury and-"

"No; fuck no," Chan interrupted with all haste, "do not go out there, Archer; I repeat, do not go out there. They can't get through the shield. We're safe; Repeat: Do not go out there."

Chan heard Archer exhale heavily into the comm as he weighed up her words.

"You sure they can't get through?" he asked at length.

"Absolutely sure - that shield is strong enough to withstand heavy weapons fire; I think it can hold off some organics pounding on it with their fists."

"Okay," came Archer's reply, "Bordello and I will stand down. What about you?"

"Me?" replied Chan with a grin Archer could not see but probably heard, "I'm going out there."

"Whoa whoa whoa, hold the fuck on a second," Archer started to protest.

"No Archer, think about it. They're right there; when will we ever get the chance to observe them again at this range, fully protected? I'm not asking for permission, Archer, I'm telling you what I'm doing."

Again, Archer did not immediately reply, but the sound of his heavy breathing from the comm told Chan that he was wrestling with a thought.

"Take a weapon, Chan," he eventually said, "non-negotiable. You observe, you record, you get the fuck back inside, okay?"

"Okay," replied Chan, secretly a little surprised that Archer had actually agreed. "See you soon."

"Oh, and Chan?" added Archer, "one more thing."

"Yeah?"

"I trust you okay? But for the love of whatever god you do or don't believe in, *don't let them in.*"

*

As promised, Chan slung a rifle over her shoulder, and hastily filled a bag with a vid recorder, a datapad, and a good, old fashioned notebook and pencil. She had no idea how long those things - *the locals* - would remain outside. Hell, she didn't even know if they would still be there when she arrived, but a surprisingly reassuring *thud* assured her that at least one of the creatures was still outside the ship.

Though she was certain that they could not penetrate the energy shield, something inside her, some base, primal instinct, warned her against lowering the main cargo ramp which would present a large and relatively defenceless point of ingress should she be proven wrong.

Don't let them in; Archer's words echoed in Chan's ears as she instead sought the narrow, single-man maintenance elevator which led from the hangar down onto the surface below. She hit the button and stepped inside. Seconds later, she was outside, her boots settling into the claggy ground beneath her. She was not wearing her helmet despite the deluge of corrosive rain which was swirling madly outside of the shield. She registered how the various foliage, and even the creatures themselves, were battered and buffeted by the noxious storm. It both fascinated and terrified her that such weather, which would spell a certain and exceedingly gruesome end for any human unfortunate enough to stumble into such a maelstrom, did not appear to be having any real effect upon neither the indigenous flora or fauna present, aside from the arguably superficial impact of the high winds.

Chan looked up, noting absently how the shield crackled and buzzed as the rain beat down upon it. She checked her datapad for a live read on the energy shield's current integrity level.

One hundred percent, she nodded emphatically as she read on the display. *I fucking told you guys.*

She stowed the datapad into her bag and took a few steps forward. A small electronic whirring noise caught her attention, and she turned to see one of the external cameras panning around to follow her movement.

Archer, she thought. *Fuck, maybe even Bordello.* She threw a mocking salute to the camera, which panned rapidly down then up, as if answering her salute with a nod of its own.

Definitely Archer. Whilst she was not surprised that the guys inside the *Jackal* were keeping a close eye on her, she was surprised to discover that this comforted her, and quite considerably. The thudding had intensified since she had stepped out onto the surface, and now that she could clearly see its origin, it made perfect sense and no sense at all.

The creatures, and a quick count revealed to Chan that there must have been around fifty of them, maybe a little more, were using the long, thin fingers which capped their forward limbs to bang on the shield the way a person might use a fist to bang earnestly upon a door. *This* explained the sound; *this* made perfect sense.

But why? Chan asked herself, as she panned her own camera around three hundred and sixty degrees, recording all of this weird and wonderful - if a little ominous - behaviour.

They aren't hostile, so they're not trying to get in and kill us.

They're clearly intelligent, so they must have realised by now that banging on the shield isn't going to do anything.

They've obviously adapted to the conditions, so they're not seeking shelter.

So what in the living fuck are they doing? This is the part which made no sense at all.

An idea came to her. It was a stupid idea, she knew, but she had seen it in at least a dozen movies so she figured it must be worth a shot.

She walked forward until her face was mere inches from the energy shield and directly in line with one of the creatures. She narrowed her eyes against the harsh yellow glare of the shield as flashes and sparks of brilliant energy flared to life outside as the rain hit the shield, casting light and shadow over her features.

She took a deep breath, and held up her right hand, slowly moving it upwards, bringing it to within mere millimetres of the shield. She waited, hand held high, fingers splayed wide. The creature on the other side of the shield seemed to consider this gesture for a moment, turning its gaze from Chan's face to her outstretched hand, then back to her face, then back to her hand. With seeming hesitation, it moved its own fingers, nervously it seemed, then raised its leftmost forward limb, spreading its own fingers wide in an exact mirror of Chan's gesture.

Chan let out an involuntary noise, halfway between a laugh and a gasp, and she clasped her left hand over her mouth as she held her right in place. The creature, too, held the pose, seemingly following Chan's lead. Sensing this, Chan moved her right arm in an arc, bringing it down from above her head ninety degrees, holding it straight out to her side, pointing to the right.

She watched in awe as the creature again followed suit, mimicking her motion.

"My god," she said out loud to nobody in particular. She had a fleeting thought that Archer and Bordello were saying the exact same thing as they watched the scene unfold on the monitors inside the Jackal.

There she stood, captivated, as the rain continued to pummel the energy shield and the wild lands of Andani beyond. But she didn't care one bit about that; she stood eye to eye with this bizarre creature, and she realised by degrees that the rhythmic thudding had stopped. She turned around to get a sense of what was happening, and was met by the sight of the creatures - all of them - watching her and one of their own communicating in their crude, rudimentary way. They had ceased pounding on the shield and were simply watching.

Chan turned back to her main subject, and noticed that it was still holding its left arm out horizontally, as she had with her right.

Okay, she thought, *what can we try next?*

A ripple of panic seemed to rumble and reverberate through the assembled crowd of creatures, and their formally relaxed and curious demeanours took on sudden yet unmistakable hues of distress and alarm. Many of them turned to flee, screeching to one another as if issuing orders, by Chan's reckoning. Chan looked here and there, trying to discern the source of such sudden and obvious alarm.

She heard an ungodly rumble, and her world turned to black.

Chapter Five

"What in the name of holy fuck?"

"Bordello, get her inside!" yelled Archer, cutting off his fellow xenoarchaeologist and gesturing wildly to the outside via the viewport. Bordello quickly nodded his understanding and ran headlong toward the nearest exit door, bracing himself against the *Jackal's* interior walls as the ship shook violently.

Archer barely heard the wailing of the alarms as he moved to the viewport to try to get a better look at what was happening out there. His eyes went wide as he saw huge cracks appearing in the mesa as the ground shook.

"Medd?" he called out over his shoulder, "anything?"

"Unprecedented tectonic activity, doctor," came the mech's matter-of-fact reply.

"I see that, Medd."

"I'm also reading massive volcanic activity on the far side of the planet. The scale of the calamity is unlike anything ever recorded on Earth, or any CSG settled worlds."

Archer spun to face the mech; his countenance was one of disbelief mingled with a dawning horror. The inner hatch opened and a gust of wind bearing an acrid, sulphurous edge blew into the ship.

"A little help?" said Bordello as he reentered. His arms were cupped beneath Chan's armpits, and his hands were tight across her chest; he was breathing heavily as he dragged her unconscious form back into the relative safety of the *Jackal*. Archer wasted no time in grabbing Chan's legs and helping Bordello place her down onto a medibench with as much care and grace as could be managed under the circumstances.

"Medd," Bordello said simply, moving out of the way so that the mech could assess and treat Chan. He *was* primarily a medical robot, after all. Satisfied that Chan was in the best - albeit mechanical - hands, Archer followed Bordello's lead and headed back to the bridge.

"What the fuck, man?" asked Bordello.

"Groundquake," replied Archer. "Significant, according to Medd. Volcanic activity, too, but not close. Did you see any of the, you know?"

"No," replied Bordello, shaking his head. "By the time I got there they were all gone."

"They seemed to…" said Archer, gesticulating as he struggled to find the right words.

"They felt it coming," Bordello offered, receiving a nod from Archer in reply. "They fucking knew. I told you, boss-man, they're fucking with us, trying to lure us outside into danger. That whole thing was a fucking *trap*."

Archer set his jaw and nodded slowly.

"I'm starting to think you might be right.

Chan groaned as Medd administered a painkiller. The sound, though small, came as a huge relief to Archer and Bordello.

"Alright," said Archer with some semblance of conviction. "Medd, get us out of here. Take off; hold at 800 metres."

"Affirmative, doctor Archer."

Within moments, Medd fired the engines, and the Crimson Jackal rose nearly a kilometre into the air, away from the destructive force of the groundquake below.

The relative stillness of the hovering ship served to calm the nerves of the two xenoarchaeologists, and Archer and Bordello slumped deeper into their respective seats with sigh of relief as the ship stabilised; the bridge was silent apart from the beeping of instruments and the hum of the engines.

The sky beyond the viewport turned a dark, inky blue, and the groundquake came to an end.

*

Morning arrived without fanfare, and all was quiet aboard the *Jackal*; Medd was inside the cockpit, busying himself with all manner of charts and readouts in order to gain a better understanding of the seismic activity they had encountered the previous night. The crew were rousing from a short but much needed sleep, and the sunlight which now shone brightly through the forward viewports lent the burgeoning day some small glimmer of positivity. Medd had brought the ship back down to the surface about two kilometres west of their original position once the worst of the storm and quake had passed, and the humans had quickly succumbed to their exhaustion, both physical and emotional. The groundquake had hit pretty badly, but the chosen landing site was as structurally sound as could be found, and this particular part of the mesa was relatively undamaged.

"Talk to me, Medd."

"Good morning Doctor Archer. Did you sleep well?"

"I mean… no, but thanks for asking. What do you have for me?"

Archer seated himself on one of the vacant cockpit flight chairs, and was joined shortly thereafter by Chan and Bordello. The aroma of hot coffee was unmistakable as it mingled with the artificial air cycled by the *Jackal's* life support systems. Bordello and Chan had arrived together, arms linked at the elbows, seemingly having put their differences aside. There was no trace of romance in the gesture, and as they took up seats of their own alongside Archer, Chan let her head fall until it rested on Bordello's shoulder.

This pleased Archer, but he did not let it show.

Like bickering siblings, those two, he thought fondly.

"Well," began Medd, "I am pleased to report that all scans point to a definitive cessation of last night's geological activities, both seismic and volcanic. In short, the worst appears to be behind us. Further, both my own and the *Crimson Jackal*'s organic sensors currently detect no trace of the indigenous creatures we have encountered. The caveat, of course, is that our respective sensor arrays are designed for decidedly shorter range tracking than we have thus far attempted."

"All good so far," offered Chan, "anything else, Medd?"

"Actually, yes," replied the mech, raising a mechanical finger for emphasis. "In our haste to gain the relative safety of a higher altitude, and our subsequent descent to a more suitable landing zone, it appears that we have, quite inadvertently, brought ourselves within actionable range of another target structure, and one of some note if I may say so."

"How noteworthy are we talking, Medd?" asked Chan, leaning forward in her seat as her interest grew.

"Well," began Medd, "it is perhaps easier to simply show you." He took out a blank datadisc and briefly touched it to a glowing panel upon the cockpit's main control array. An accompanying *beep* told the mech that the data had successfully been transferred to the disc. He held his hand out, palm up, and thumbed the activation button. A green, glowing, wireframe image sprung to life in the air, and the three humans gasped, wide-eyed, as they beheld the slowly rotating holographic image.

"You've gotta be fucking kidding me," said Bordello.

"No," said Chan, shaking her head, "that's not possible."

"Medd," added Archer, "are you sure this hasn't been - I don't know - *corrupted* somehow? Tampered with?"

"Quite sure, sir," replied Medd, simply. "The data is accurate, Doctors; the structure you are looking at lies less than four kilometres due-west of our current location."

The trio continued to stare in disbelief at the holo-image, and Chan stood to get a better look as she walked a circle around the glowing representation before them.

It showed a large, flat plain, upon which stood a ring of enormous standing stones. Though many of the stones had fallen or been damaged over time, most of the structure remained intact. It consisted of pairs of vertical stones, some thirty feet high and at least ten feet wide, capped with equally commanding lintel stones. These pairs of capped vertical stones repeated themselves in a large circular formation, creating a stone circle which must easily have been over two hundred feet in diameter. At the centre of the imposing circle was a set of smaller stones, laid flat upon the ground in a pattern whose significance was not immediately apparent.

Whilst the stone circle itself was undoubtedly impressive - even in holographic form - something else about it was deeply unsettling, and each of the three humans felt a certain disquiet, a feeling of uneasy dread at the sheer and undeniable *familiarity* of it.

"What the fuck is it?" mumbled Bordello, essentially to himself.

"This, Doctors," announced Medd, choosing to answer the clearly rhetorical question, "is our next destination of interest."

"Hold up a second," said Archer. "I thought we had agreed to return to the monolith."

"After what happened there?" Chan replied, "I'd suggest we make do with the data we already have."

"I agree," said Bordello. "We don't know what might be waiting for us here," he said, pointing to Medd's slowly revolving holomap, "but we know exactly what's waiting for us back there."

*

The day was still young when the lander departed the *Jackal,* and though Andani's sun was rapidly approaching its zenith, a moody, ominous quiet hung over the lands beyond. The crew had geared up and joined Medd in the hangar not thirty minutes after the mech had shown them the holographic representation of the stone circle, such was their interest in the structure and their determination to press on with their mission, despite the events of the past day or two.

"How much longer, Medd?" called Bordello from the seat behind the driving mech.

"We should establish visual contact with the structure within three minutes, Doctor, but I believe we may have a problem." A collective groan emanated from the lander's three human occupants.

"What *now*, Medd?" demanded Archer, as the lander continued to hurtle at pace across the uneven ground, causing its occupants to jolt and sway, here and there, in tandem with their passage across the unpredictable terrain.

"It would appear, according to our sensors, that the tectonic activity we encountered last night has opened up something of a crevasse which lies directly in our path."

"Passable?" asked Chan.

"Negative, at least for the lander," replied Medd.

"We should have come in the *Jackal*," offered Bordello, receiving nods of agreement in response, including from their mech driver.

"We'll assess the situation once we have boots on the ground," said Archer, motioning for calm, "let's not get ahead of ourselves."

The pitch of the lander's engines began to recede, and the landscape speeding by beyond the viewports began to slow as Medd brought the lander to a stop.

"We are here," announced the mech, somewhat needlessly. The crew unstrapped themselves from their seats without delay, and Archer moved to pull open the lander door. He hesitated, and turned to face their mech.

"Medd, did the quake kick up anything we should know about?"

"How do you mean, Doctor Archer?"

"The air; are we gonna step outside here into some noxious smog cloud or something?"

"No, sir. All scans report no changes to the quality, nor indeed the chemical composition, of the air. It is quite safe to breathe unassisted. Our main concern is merely the distance we must travel on foot. I cannot take the lander beyond this point as the terrain simply does not allow for it."

Nodding, Archer threw open the door and stepped out, leaving his helmet behind; Chan and Bordello followed him, their helmets, too, remaining safely ensconced within the lander.

"Holy fuck," remarked Bordello as he turned to gaze west. Even at this distance, a good kilometre or more from the imposing stone structure, its sheer scale and the power it seemed to exude as it stood stoically on the other side of the crevasse were mesmerising; it was at once a majestic and deeply unsettling sight.

"Remind you of anything?" Bordello continued, giving Archer a quick nudge.

"Don't say it, man. Don't even say it," replied the older of the two xenoarchaeologists, "it's just not fucking possible."

The quartet began their slow, purposeful walk; it was a good distance from the lander to the crevasse, upon whose western side the structure stood. A long march in a somewhat contemplative silence eventually brought them to the great chasm which had been carved into the very rock beneath their feet by the groundquake. They edged forward slowly, stepping tentatively to the edge of the precipice, watching their footing and checking their balance as they went; the last thing they needed was for the ground to crumble beneath their boots and send them down into the depths of fuck-knows-what.

"Well, we tried," said Bordello with a resigned sigh.

"What do you mean?" Chan answered, brow furrowed in confusion. By way of an answer, Bordello gestured broadly at the crevasse which lay before them.

"This," he replied with a wave of his arm, "it's gotta be thirty metres to the other side."

"Twenty-seven-point-six," added Medd.

"Exactly," Bordello continued, "we can't cross this. We have to abort."

"Cut the shit, Bordello," said Archer, a little more sharply than he had intended, "our short-range jump packs will clear that with room to spare."

"Fuck that," Bordello answered. "You're not getting me to jump over a fucking endless chasm on a fucked up alien planet; nah-ah," he added, shaking his head for emphasis.

"Come on, man," added Chan, wearily, "don't be a pussy; we can easily make that jump."

"Fuck you; I aint doing it," Bordello said with unmistakeable finality, going as far as crossing his arms for emphasis.

"Fine," said Archer with a heavy sigh. "Stay here and guard the lander. Medd, Chan, follow me."

Archer did not look at Bordello as he stalked away, shaking his head in frustration. The biologist and the mech followed Archer as he skirted the edge of the enormous fissure hewn into the very rock by the groundquake. He found a suitable spot, a place where the distance between their side and the side which housed the ominous stone circle was at its shortest.

"On three, okay?" receiving nods in reply, he continued. "One, two, three."

The jump packs emitted a low *whoosh* as their boosters fired, sending Archer, Chan, and Medd some fifteen feet into the air at high velocity. As Archer had stated, the jump packs did indeed pack sufficient punch to see the trio safely to the other side with minimal effort. Once they touched down gently on the other side, Archer spared a quick glance over his shoulder, seeking for Bordello but finding his fellow archaeologist already heading back to the lander.

Fuck him, thought Archer. *Fucking coward.*

"Come on," he said simply, motioning for Chan and Medd to follow him. They moved forward up a shallow incline littered with rocks and boulders of the same red stone which was ubiquitous across the entire visible landscape. They were not yet amongst the imposing stones, yet the structure loomed large in the near distance, standing like a silent guardian of some unseen ancient power. The trio pushed on through the rough terrain, and finally found themselves at the site of the towering stone circle.

"My god…" said Chan, as she craned her neck to take in the colossal stones.

"Look at the size of these things," added Archer, equally awestruck. "What in all the worlds could possibly have made this?"

"I believe, Doctors," said Medd, "that is precisely what we are here to find out."

Chapter Six

"Hey, Archer; do you read me? Over."

Archer took a moment to compose himself before answering the radio.

"Copy, Bordello. What's the view like from the monitors? Over."

"Your vitals all look good; slightly elevated heart rates, but that's to be expected, right? Hey, what are those things, boss-man? Over."

"As soon as *we* know, *you'll* know. Over and out." Archer took up a position at the base of the nearest stone, with Chan and Medd each picking a different stone and doing the same.

"My god," said Chan under her breath as she removed one of her gloves and touched the cold, rough surface of the enormous stone which stood before her. "Hey, Medd?"

"Yes, Doctor Chan?"

"What do you make of these markings?" Chan gestured to the intricate, seemingly runic carvings upon the stone column. Just like those upon the towering monolith which the group had inspected what felt like a lifetime ago, the markings they now beheld, too, were glowing faintly.

"Well, upon an initial, somewhat cursory inspection, my conclusion would be that these are very similar to the carvings we have previously catalogued."

"Similar?" interjected Archer, walking over to Chan and Medd, "they look identical to me."

"A perfectly reasonable assessment for a human to make, my good doctor, but there is a certain, subtle difference which would perhaps be more obvious to a graphologist than a scientist."

"*Graphologist?*" echoed Chan. "Are you saying there is a difference in, what, *handwriting?*"

"To the layman, yes," replied Medd. "I cannot be certain without performing a series of tests back on the *Crimson Jackal*, but an initial comparison of the glyphs at the two sites we have visited thus far reveals clear and obvious differences."

"Such as?" added Archer when the mech did not elaborate.

"Well, Doctor, the glyphs we recorded at the first site were somewhat elegant in their creation; they displayed a certain degree of control and finesse. I believe that this is indicative of time and care having been taken in the carving of the symbols."

"Okay, so what about these?" asked Chan, gesturing to the stone in front of her.

"These," Medd replied, "appear to have been carved with somewhat less care and attention. Note here - the rough edges and uneven curves - this speaks of a more hurried application by a more unsteady hand. To conclude, I would suggest that this is indicative of-"

"Panic," Archer finished for the mech.

"Indeed, Doctor."

"Are we any closer to translating any of this, Medd?" asked Chan, trying to force away a sickly, gnawing dread which was just beginning to announce itself in the pit of her stomach.

"I'm afraid not," replied the mech, "but the data is still being scrutinised by the systems aboard the ship.

We should know more very soon, especially once we add this new data to the existing information."

"Well let's get to it then," said Archer, trying to reimpose a degree of urgency. He, Chan, and Medd took out an assortment of recording and scanning devices, and set about making as detailed a recording of the stone circle and the strange, glowing markings as they could while the light still held sway.

It had turned cold, though Archer and Chan were too busy to really notice it, and thick clouds had begun to gather overhead. A brief but intense flash, somewhere off in the distance to the east spoke of a burgeoning storm upon the horizon, but still the trio worked, moving amongst the colossal stones with recorders in hand, afraid to miss even a single detail.

"Uh, guys?" came a crackly voice from both Archer and Chan's radios.

"We're kinda busy here, Bordello; can it wait? Over," said Chan.

"You got a storm moving in fast; rain, and lots of it, over."

Archer and Chan looked at each other in alarm, and Archer thumbed the radio.

"The corrosive kind or the normal kind? Over."

"Uh, as far as I can tell from this data, it's just the normal kind, but I still think you'd better get back here. Over."

"I agree with Doctor Bordello," stated Medd. "We do not want to get caught outside in the midst of a storm."

As if on cue, the rain began to fall.

"Alright," said Archer, "pack it up. We'll head back. Bordello?" he added, raising the radio to his mouth, "prep the lander. We'll be there in-"

"Shit! Fuck! Shit! Guys, we've got company!" came Bordello's frantic voice over the radio.

"Repeat, over!" demanded Archer.

"Locals, Archer, those fucking creatures! They're heading right for us at speed. Over."

"Fuck," snapped Archer. "How many? And which direction are they coming from?"

"Hundreds, boss-man. Thousands maybe, and they're not coming *in*, they're coming *up* - out of the fucking ground, man!"

The creatures were close, climbing vertically, scaling the wall of the crevasse, crawling up from the bowels of the planet toward the surface.

"Say again Bordello - I can't hear you. There's too much interference, over."

"Can you hear me, Archer? Get the fuck out of there!"

"Fuck - I can't hear you, Bordello!"

"Fuck this," Bordello said aloud to nobody, and he slammed the now useless radio down onto the metal floor of the lander. He ran straight for the door and did not break stride as he made footfall on the surface, running out into the driving rain. He quickly made it to the edge of the deep crevasse and, not knowing what else to do, he began to jump up and down on the spot, waving his arms frantically above his head as he did so in a last-ditch attempt to alert his friends to the danger they were in.

"Hey!" he shouted, struggling to make himself heard over the deluge which now poured openly from the dark skies. "Fuck it," Bordello said under his breath, before removing a phosphorous flare from his kit belt. He lit it without delay, and frantically waved it over his head.

It worked, at the sight of the glowing red flame, Archer, Chan, and Medd turned and faced Bordello's direction.

"The fuck is he doing?" asked Archer, trying to suppress the panic which was beginning to well up inside his chest.

"Bordello?" he said into the radio, receiving only static in return.

"I don't like this, Archer," said Chan, a slight edge of fear tinging her voice, "maybe we should-"

She left her sentence hanging in the air, unfinished, as she opened her eyes wide and gasped in disbelief. The creatures, the *locals*, were spilling out of the chasm in their hundreds, alighting on Bordello's side of the great divide.

The xenoarchaeologist never stood a chance.

Archer, Chan, and Medd could only watch on in horror as the creatures quickly surrounded the hapless Bordello.

"No!" came the collective cry from the trio on the safe side of the chasm as they beheld one of the creatures reaching out and grasping Bordello by the top of the head, its long, sickly fingers gripping his cheeks. Bordello's eyes quickly lost focus, and his jaw dropped, as if a great shock had befallen him, or some great revelation had been laid bare by the locals.

A solitary tear escaped his eye, and rolled slowly down his cheek as he stood, transfixed and immobilised by the creature in whose grasp he found himself.

"What the fuck do we do?" asked Archer.

"I do not believe there is much we *can* do," replied Medd.

Before any of them could speak again, the creature let go of Bordello and took a step back from the still dazed scientist.

"Bordello!" Archer screamed into the radio, "Bordello, do you copy? Fuck, speak to me, man!"

Though the rain and environmental interference rendered Archer's words into nothing but a static haze, the noise at least served to bring some semblance of focus back to Bordello's eyes. He looked at Archer, locking eyes with the older scientist, some thirty metres away, through the relentless downpour. He held his friend, his *mentor's* gaze for a long, tense, agonising moment, before speaking two short, quick words which were lost to the elements, unheard amid the din of the wind and driving rain.

Averting his eyes, and taking a single, long stride forward, he allowed himself to fall into the chasm.

I'm sorry.

*

It was a standoff; Archer, Chan, and Medd stood upon the western edge of the chasm, whilst the great throng of creatures held the eastern edge. Not a soul among them moved. The creatures stood, hissing and snarling, staring at the two humans and the mech, but making no move to cross the divide or otherwise accost the trio. Of them, Archer and Chan stared with unfocused eyes at the spot in the chasm into which Bordello had fallen.

No, thought Archer, *not fallen - jumped.*

"Doctors?"

The sound of Medd's insistent electronic voice served to snap Archer back to his senses, and he turned his back to the creatures to face Medd and Chan.

"We've gotta go," he said simply. "We have to get out of here."

Medd nodded his agreement, but Chan did not reply. Unlike Archer, she had not yet fully regained her wits, such was the state of shock in which she found herself.

"Chan?" Archer said, in a gentle yet unmistakably urgent tone. She did not immediately answer, but her eyes moved to meet his, and Archer registered a low, aching feeling in his stomach as he beheld both the look and the tears in Chan's eyes.

She's losing it, he concluded.

Much more of this and her mind will be lost.

"Chan," he said again, taking her gently by the shoulders, "we're dying out here. We have to go."

At this, Chan stirred, slowly coming back to her senses and nodding her own agreement.

"It has to be unanimous," she whispered, more to herself than her companions. "Get us out of here, Medd."

"And how exactly is he going to do that if we can't even get to the lander?" asked Archer, indicating the swarming mass of creatures between them and the lander, saying nothing of the deep, black chasm at their feet.

"The packs," Chan replied. "We use the jump packs to get behind them; once we hit the ground, we drop everything we can and run for the lander."

"Chan," Archer began, "I don't think-"

"Doctor Chan is quite right, sir," added Medd. "The jump packs should have sufficient power to take us beyond the line of the creatures by, according to my projections, some twenty metres."

Archer took a deep breath and chewed the idea over for barely a moment, before he set his jaw and nodded tersely.

"It'll be close," he said, "and we'll only get one chance. No mistakes, okay?"

The trio each took a moment to compose themselves, eyes constantly darting toward the creatures, alert for any change in their behaviour, before steeling themselves for what was to come.

"On three, okay?" said Archer, receiving nods in reply.

"Okay… One, two, THREE!"

The jump packs engaged in unison, and three glowing orange trails, sailing high above the heads of the onlooking creatures, heralded the success of the trio's plan.

They hit the ground at a run, simultaneously unhooking straps and unclipping belts, discarding anything which was not absolutely essential to their survival in order to make themselves as light and as fast as possible.

The lander was ahead, visible in the near distance; a safe haven they were desperate to reach if only their legs could carry them beyond its threshold. It was still a long way off, but Archer, Medd, and Chan spared nothing as they ran, acutely aware of the rumble and snarls which signalled that the undulating mass of creatures had given chase.

Whether born of some form of intuition, some undefined, nebulous sixth-sense, or whether it was merely a function of his primary senses being in a state of hypervigilance, Archer suddenly became aware that Chan had stopped running. He dared to risk a glance over his shoulder, and his eyes went wide as he watched Chan come to a halt, stopping and turning to face the creatures as they pawed and skittered toward her in their masses.

"Chan!" he screamed, unable to formulate anything more coherent or useful.

Chan turned her head and met his gaze; her eyes were clear, and Archer could read determination and clarity of purpose in her countenance.

"I have to know," she said simply, before turning back to face the creatures once more.

Archer's hand went instinctively to his hip, reaching for the sidearm he had discarded as he ran, along with any and every other item he could possibly have utilised as a weapon. Chan, for her part, had kept a flare in her belt, and it was this she now drew and struck, bathing the scene in a neon fuschia, brilliant despite the ongoing downpour. She cast it behind her, between herself and the watching Archer and Medd. The creatures were now upon her, and the ones in the lead hissed angrily and averted their eyes from the glowing flare.

Good, thought Chan, *they don't like the flare. Just as I had hoped. All animals retreat from fire.*

No sooner had this thought coalesced in her mind than a strong, alien hand reached out and grabbed her by the head.

Her eyes went wide and her jaw hung open.

In her mind, Chan was transported to another place, in another time. Her mind was aflame with colours, sounds, and images she could not make sense of. She saw fire. She saw destruction. She saw death. Death, but not just of beings, creatures, populaces; she saw the deaths of entire planets and entire star systems, all across space and time.

Her mind seemed to focus, to lose some of the hazy edges and chaotic dissonance, and she saw the monoliths, stone circles, and monuments of this world. She saw alien hands carving indecipherable symbols, glyphs, and runes; day in, day out, for centuries, these alien hands left their marks upon the towering structures, but for a purpose Chan did not yet understand; that she had not yet been *shown*.

The images which raced across her mind narrowed, honing in on the carvings themselves, still so utterly alien to Chan. But then they seemed to shift, to move, to resolve themselves into something, some variation of a language that Chan could understand to a degree.

The symbols became numbers in her mind's eye, and the seemingly arbitrary patterns became perfectly ordered sequences.

Numbers, sequences, patterns… No, not just numbers, *dates*.

Millennia, centuries, decades, years, months, weeks, days, hours, and minutes… A countdown. A countdown to…

Through the sheer application of a will which Chan did not know she was possessed of, she forcibly regained some semblance of control and struggled loose of the creature's grasp, breaking its connection to her mind. The creature recoiled, as if its fingers had been burned by an unseen flame, and Chan clutched her head, trying to soothe the pain which the unscheduled severing of the mind-meld had induced. Ignoring the blood which fell openly from her nose and eye sockets, she turned to Archer, finding his desperate and pleading eyes through the dying glow of the neon flare amongst the rain.

"Go," she said simply, before collapsing to the ground.

Chapter Seven

Archer knew that the dying flare would not keep the creatures at bay for much longer and so, despite his horror and grief, and despite every sense of moral duty within him screaming that he should try to help Chan somehow, if she was even still alive, he turned and ran for the safety of the lander with Medd falling in step right beside him.

They made it to the lander with the creatures on their heels, and neither man nor mech spoke as muscle-memory kicked in and they fell into their respective roles; Archer slammed and sealed the door, taking a weapon from the rack as he secured himself into his seat. He trained the rifle's sights on the door as Medd, wasting no time, entered the driver's seat and fired up the engines.

With a deep mechanical roar, the lander burst into motion, heading directly back toward the *Crimson Jackal*, its two occupants very much aware that the teeming mass of creatures had not yet given up the chase and were actively pursuing them across the desolate Andanian plains. The lander, though, was too fast for the creatures, and they soon fell behind and out of sight of both human eye and short range sensors.

"There," Archer said, pointing out of the forward viewport as the *Jackal* came into view; a welcome sight it was to Archer's broken and traumatised mind. Medd did not acknowledge Archer's exclamation, but continued to manoeuvre the lander deftly across the terrain toward their target. When they were within two hundred metres of the ship, Medd hit a button on the centre console, and Archer punched the air in an emphatic demonstration of relief as he watched the Jackal's landing ramp descend invitingly; the artificial light emanating from inside the hangar had never looked so good.

Within moments, the lander was inside, and Medd hit another button which remotely closed the landing ramp behind them. Neither man nor mech spoke as they raced from the lander out into the hangar, and then upwards for the sanctity of the main decks of the ship.

"Okay Medd, get us out of here."

"Affirmative, Doctor. Hailing the *Imperious* now."

Medd took a command key from its position upon the main console, and plugged it into a red-and-yellow chevroned SOS receiver. He entered a string of commands, and hit 'send'.

"I have informed the *Imperious* of our *situation*, Doctor, and requested that we exit this system the moment the *Jackal* has docked."

"Good work, Medd. Which command override did you use?"

"Override 22-1-B, sir."

"Shit, okay. Man, will I have some explaining to do."

"I thought it most succinctly captured the essence of our crisis, doctor."

Archer merely nodded; command override 22-1-B was serious, rarely utilised except in the most dire of emergencies. Archer was already considering how he was going to explain this to CSG command, when a beeping noise sounded from the console, and a small green light began to flash.

"What's that, Medd?"

"The data, sir," replied Medd, already reaching across to access the files and stop the beeping and flashing, "the analysis of the carvings is complete." The mech entered a command on the console, and a holographic readout was projected into the air between Medd and Archer, casting their faces in an otherworldly red glow.

"Well, what does it say?" asked Archer impatiently. The *Jackal* broke through the last vestiges of Andani's atmosphere, and the forward viewport was now a tapestry of star-mottled darkness, but for the utilitarian grey shape of the *Imperious* which hung invitingly before them.

"It would appear, sir," Medd began, "that the symbols are… oh my."

Archer raised his eyebrows and leaned forward.

"Medd, what is it? Tell me."

"It would appear, sir, that the carvings were some form of… *calendar,* you might say; a method of recording a decreasing numerical sequence.."

"Decreasing sequence? What the fuck are you talking about, Medd?" snapped Archer.

"A *countdown*, Doctor Archer."

"A countdown? A countdown to *what*, Medd?" asked Archer, vaguely aware that he already knew the answer.

"To *death*, sir. To the death of the planet," the mech said with an uncanny facsimile of human emotion present in its artificial voice. Archer was silent for a long moment as he tried to reconcile Medd's words.

"What about the creatures," he began, "do we know anything more about them?"

"The creatures, it seems, were responsible for the carvings - ancestrally speaking. I believe, sir, that Doctor Chan was quite right as regards their intentions."

"What do you mean? Right about what?"

"The creatures, sir. They knew what was coming, and they knew when it would - *will* - happen. They were not trying to harm us, sir, they were trying to *warn* us."

*

The *Crimson Jackal* docked with the *Imperious* with little fanfare, and the capital ship's acceptance of

Medd's command override code ensured that the *Imperious* remained in the Fomori cluster not a moment longer than necessary following the successful docking of Archer and Medd's ship. With a blinding light and a deep rumble of its hyper-powered *Newtondrive* engines, the *Imperious* blink-skipped away from the system.

Only silence followed in its wake; a deep, throbbing silence which hung over the planet Andani like a dark veil. Time seemed to stretch inexorably into an empty nothingness, though, by the reckoning of humans, only a few hours had passed since the *Imperious* had fled the system.

Without warning, without herald, and with no final, elaborate flourish as the curtain fell, the planet Andani crumbled and burned.

*

Boom, boom, boom, went the drum.

Thud, thud, thud; its echo reverberated across all of existence, past, present, and future.

The ripples in the very fabric of space and time were distorted at the rhythmic beating of the great drum; their wavelengths increasing, stretching exponentially just for a moment, as a small, backwater planet in a distant, barely explored system on the other side of the universe died.

Boom, boom, boom, went the drum, and somewhere, in some unseen, unknowable corner, deep in the vast and unimaginable darkness of space, something laughed.

Printed in Great Britain
by Amazon